This Little Tiger book belongs to:

_____

_____

_____

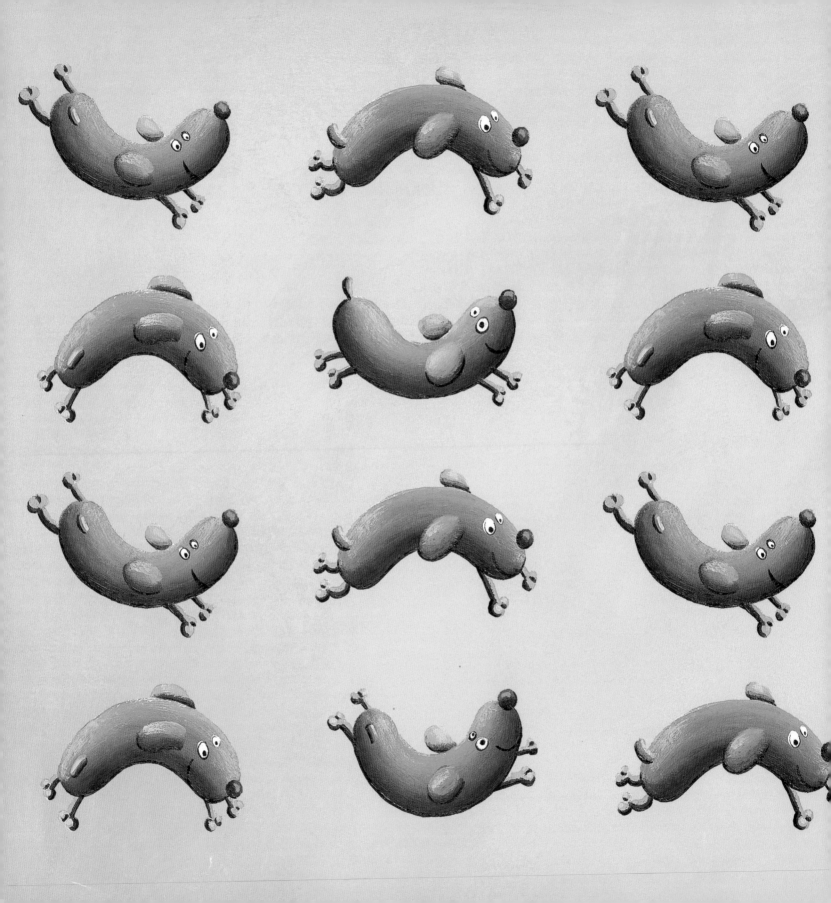

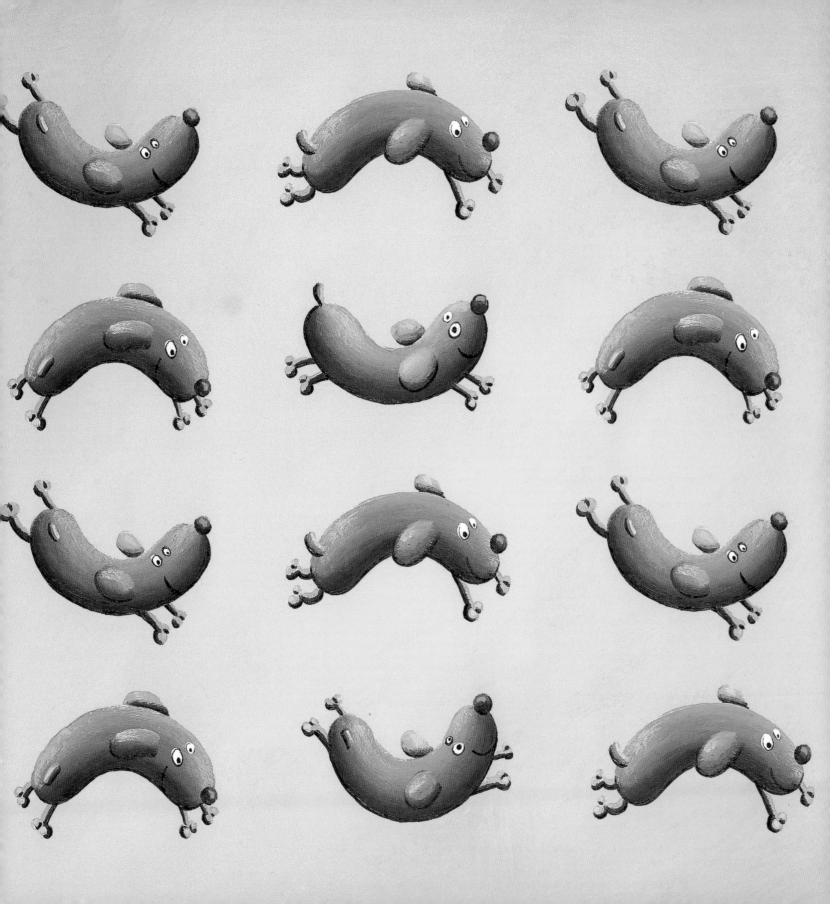

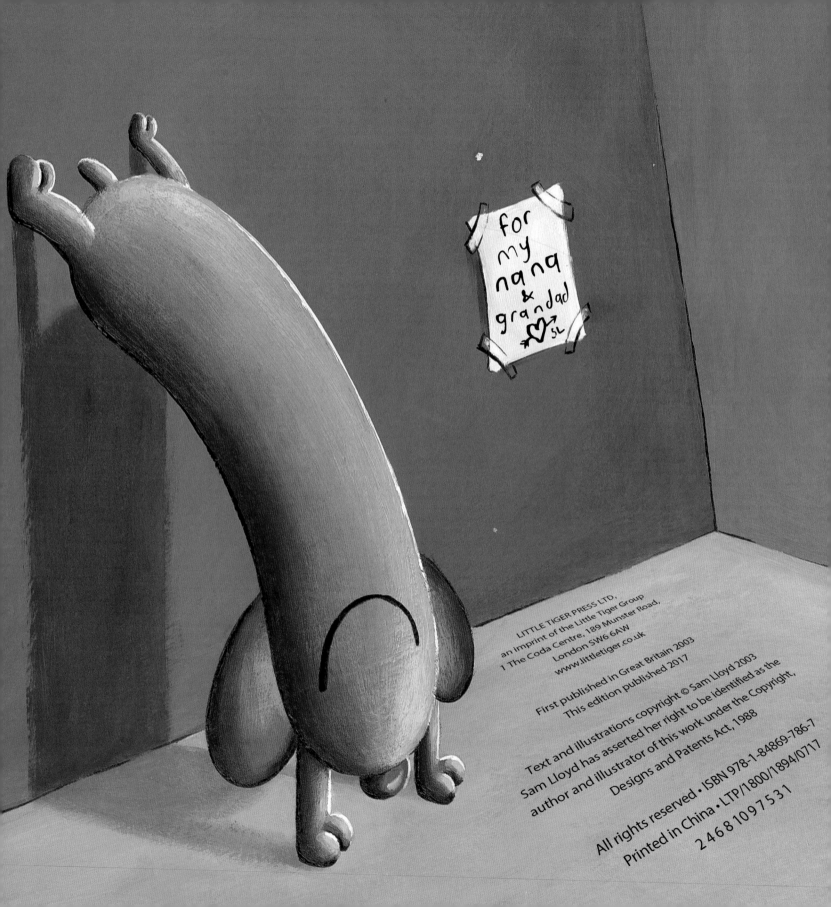

for
my
nana
&
grandad
SL

LITTLE TIGER PRESS LTD,
an imprint of the Little Tiger Group
1 The Coda Centre, 189 Munster Road,
London SW6 6AW
www.littletiger.co.uk

First published in Great Britain 2003
This edition published 2017

SUPER SID

THE SILLY SAUSAGE DOG

by

Sam Lloyd

LITTLE TIGER

LONDON

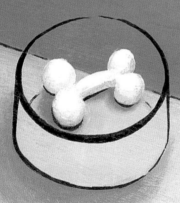

Sid was a sausage dog who lived in the kennels on the edge of town. He lived there because he didn't have a nice kind owner to love and care for him like other dogs.

Sid wanted a nice kind
owner more than
anything. So he decided
to find one for himself!

First Sid took a giant leap over the kennel wall, to show what a good jumper he was . . .

But . . .

. . . he landed on top
of Madam Murples'
very fancy tea party.

"Silly Sid!"
screeched the ladies.
"Back to the kennels
at once!"

Then Sid tried to show everyone what a good digger he was.

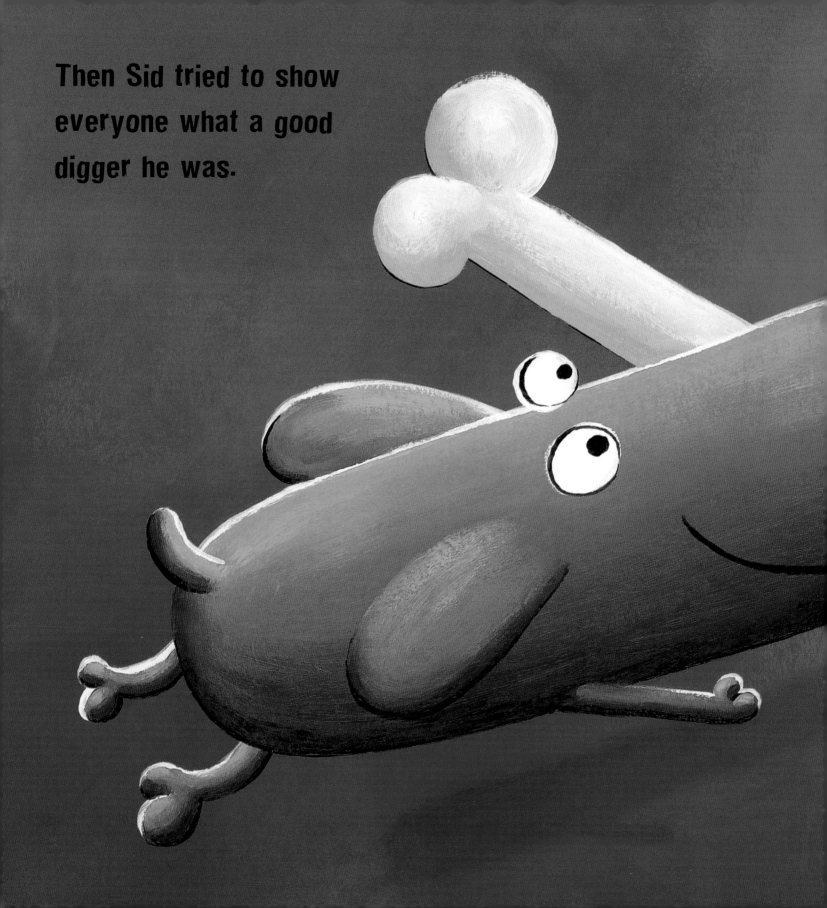

But . . .

. . . he dug up all Gardener
Pete's prize vegetables.

"**Silly Sid!**" growled Pete. "Now I'll never win the best vegetable competition. Back to the kennels with you!"

"I know," thought Sid. "I'll show
everyone what a good singer I am.
That will cheer them up."
He howled and howled as loud as
his doggy lungs would let him.

aaOOOOOOOOOOOW!

But . . . .

. . . he woke the whole street!
"SILLY SID!"
they cried, throwing water at him.
"Go away!"

Poor Sid. Sad, wet and lonely
he crept back to the kennels.
"Nobody wants me," he thought.
"I'll never find a proper home."

The next morning Sid was wakened by a very

strange smell. He put his nose into the air and, without thinking, he followed the smell . . . .

...out the window, across the yard, over the wall, under the fence, through the garden, around the bird table until at last he came to . . .

. . . A FIRE!

Little Billy's dinner was on fire.

Grandma had forgotten all about it.

aaOOOOOOOOW!

Sid jumped up and down and he sang and he woofed. And he howled as loud as his doggy lungs would let him. Until . . .

. . . the firefighter came and,
with a rush and a gush and
a great big splash, he put
the fire *out*!

"Clever Sid," said Grandma.
"Brave Sid," said the firefighter.
"Super Sid," said the crowd.

"My Sid!" said Little Billy.

So Sid had found not one but two of the nicest, kindest owners **ever!**

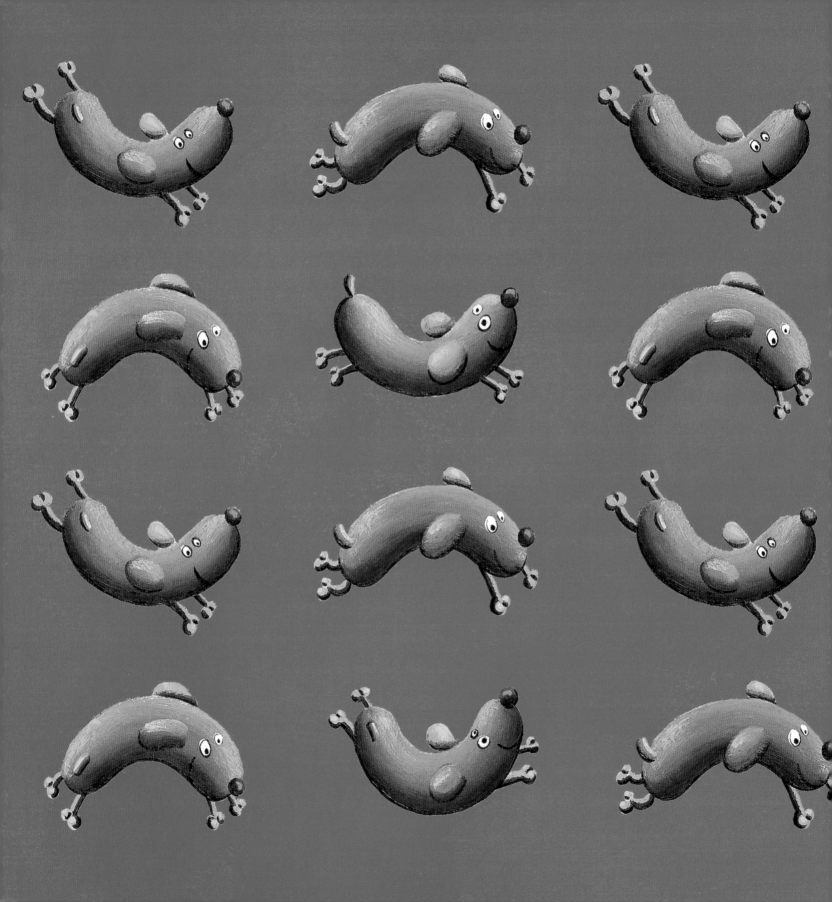

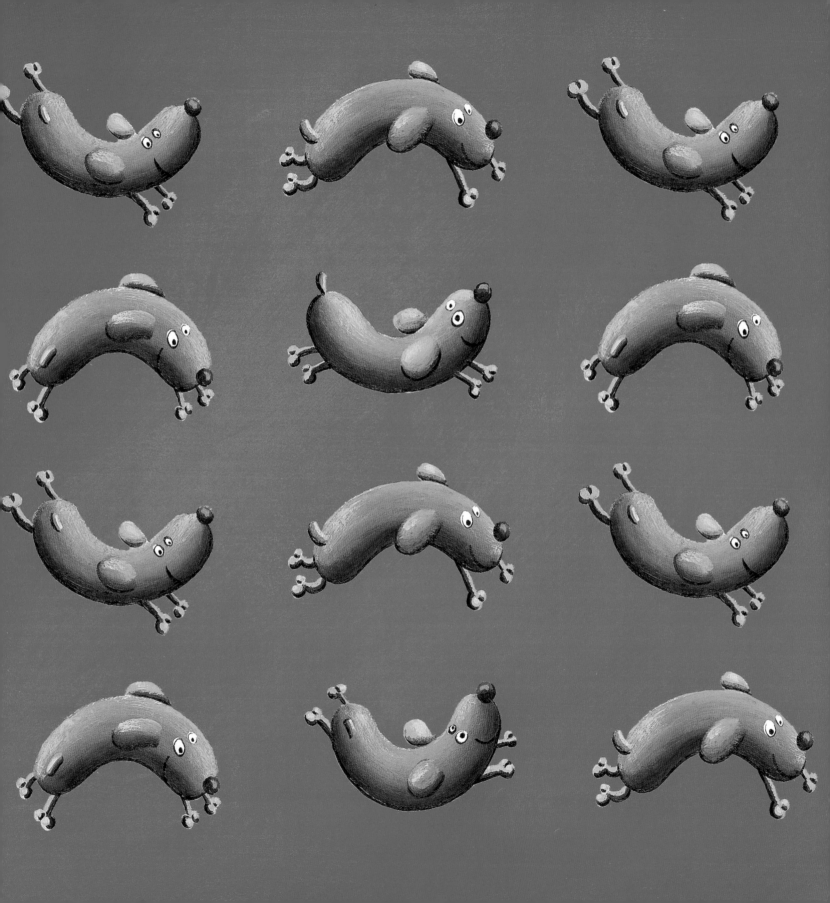